Surprise Party Surprise

Adapted by **Steve Behling**
Based on the episode written by **Mike Kubat**
Designed by **David Roe**

Los Angeles • New York

It is Ghost-Spider's birthday.

Spidey and Miles
plan a party.

Iron Man helps.

Ms. Marvel helps.

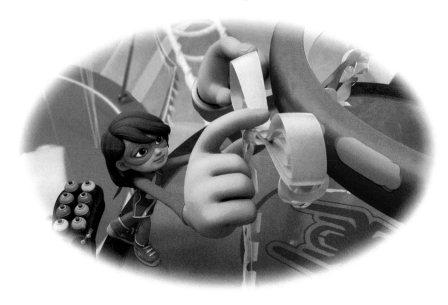

Black Panther helps.

Hulk helps, too!

It is party time!

Let's go!

Uh-oh! It is Rhino!

Stop right there, big guy!

Rhino runs.

The spiders stop him.

It is party time!

What is that?

Let's find out!

Uh-oh! It is Electro!

Stop, Electro!

She gets away!

Ghost-Spider stops her.

She gets Electro.

Uh-oh! It is Green Goblin!

"We can help," Iron Man says.

Black Cat steals a necklace.

Sandman makes a mess.

But help is here!

Iron Man gets Sandman.

Black Panther and Ms. Marvel stop Black Cat.

Spidey chases Gobby.

The webs trap him.

The heroes save the day!

Now it is time for fun.

What a great day!